Hope is the Thing with Feathers

PRAISE FOR *STORYSHARES*

"One of the brightest innovators and game-changers in the education industry."
– Forbes

"Your success in applying research-validated practices to promote literacy serves as a valuable model for other organizations seeking to create evidence-based literacy programs."

- Library of Congress

"We need powerful social and educational innovation, and Storyshares is breaking new ground. The organization addresses critical problems facing our students and teachers. I am excited about the strategies it brings to the collective work of making sure every student has an equal chance in life."
– Teach For America

"Around the world, this is one of the up-and-coming trailblazers changing the landscape of literacy and education."
- International Literacy Association

"It's the perfect idea. There's really nothing like this. I mean wow, this will be a wonderful experience for young people."   - Andrea Davis Pinkney, Executive Director, Scholastic

"Reading for meaning opens opportunities for a lifetime of learning. Providing emerging readers with engaging texts that are designed to offer both challenges and support for each individual will improve their lives for years to come. Storyshares is a wonderful start."
- David Rose, Co-founder of CAST & UDL

Hope is the Thing with Feathers

Hailey Hudson

STORYSHARES

Story Share, Inc.
New York. Boston. Philadelphia

Storyshares
Story Share, Inc.
24 N. Bryn Mawr Avenue #340
Bryn Mawr, PA 19010-3304
www.storyshares.org

Inspiring reading with a new kind of book.

Interest Level: Middle School
Grade Level Equivalent: 4.5

9781642611564

Book design by Storyshares

Printed in the United States of America

Storyshares Presents

Hope is the Thing with Feathers

There is a bird outside my window. I lean on the sill and let the cool air, just beginning to feel like spring, caress my face. I peer up through the leaves and smile at the bird. He is a swallow, I think. I like birds; I have always liked birds. My middle name, Zipporah, comes from the Hebrew word meaning bird. But Tata told me today that I must not tell anyone my middle name. I don't know why.

Amlie Zipporah Chladek. That is my name. I listen to the swallow singing, his voice soaring up and down, higher than he flies. His feathers are bluer than the sky, and they shine in the sun. I think happily about the trip Andrej, my brother, has promised me. I have just turned eight and he says he'll take me with him on an adventure throughout Prague, the city where we live. I don't know where, but anywhere with Andrej is sure to be wonderful. Soon he will be fourteen.

"For Andrej's birthday, Mama and Tata are giving him a new bicycle!" I tell the swallow. But the moment I have said this, I wish I had not. At the sound of my voice, the swallow leaps into frightened flight, so quickly that I do not realize he is gone until I see him rise above the trees. He circles once, warbles down at me, and flies away. The spring air flows across my face and the windowsill is cool on my elbows.

That Perches in the Soul

    I am burrowed under my covers, curled into a tiny ball, my nose touching my knees. I poke my head over the top of my blankets and see the streetlights shining outside my window. The water flowing down the glass makes them look funny; the gold color of the light is all blurred. Spring is almost here, but for tonight it is rainy and cold again. I huddle back down and give a little contented sigh because my bed is so warm and lovely, and I am tired and almost asleep. Somewhere, perhaps in the apartment above us, soft music is playing.

"You can't publish that!"

Drowsily, I hear Mama's voice floating down the hallway.

"Petra, don't worry." That's Tata, my strong and wonderful father, who works for a newspaper. The corners of my mouth turn up just from hearing his voice. It sounds like the water running over my windowpane, gently soothing and comforting.

"You know what they're doing to Jews. We can't give the Germans another reason to target us!" Mama's voice is just the opposite of Tata's. She sounds nervous and angry, as she usually does.

My legs are beginning to hurt. I stretch them out, but not so far that my toes come out from under my blankets. I can hear Tata's voice coming in a gentle stream from the kitchen, but I can't make out his words.

I'm almost asleep when Mama says sharply, "I told you two years ago, when the Germans invaded in 1939. It's bad enough that you're a Jew, worse still that you work for a newspaper and openly oppose the Nazis. I dont know why we've lasted this long. I should have listened to my mother, who told me not to marry a Jew..."

Tata speaks again, indistinguishably. A chair scrapes back violently and footsteps tap harshly away.

The rain taps softly on my window. I nestle under the covers and fall asleep.

Hope is the Thing with Feathers

And Sings the Tune Without the Words

I skip down the sidewalk, feeling the warm cobblestones through the bottom of my worn-out shoes. Summer has come to Prague. I tip my head back and look up to the top of our building, smiling at the birds wheeling in the sky as they sing gaily. The world is bright, beautiful, and full of joy.

Hearing footsteps behind me, I turn around. My smile grows. Hana and Magda, two of my good friends from school, are coming towards me. I have not seen them in a long time.

I expect them to stop and play. Surely they have nothing they must do on this beautiful summer afternoon, when all of Prague is in the streets despite the German soldiers at every corner. But they walk past me. They do not even look at me.

"Hana," I say, low. Confused. I lick my lips and try again, louder. "Magda. Where are you going? I've missed you!"

Hana turns around, tossing her blond braids over her shoulder. When we were younger, I was always envious of her blond curls, wishing I could trade my own dark locks for a lighter color. "We dont play with Jew-pigs," she says haughtily.

The world stops spinning. I hear nothing but her voice. My birds have disappeared, and I no longer feel the ground beneath my feet. All I can see is her blond hair, shining as brightly as the summer sun.

Magda deliberately leans forward and spits on the cobblestones at my feet.

They turn and walk away.

Feeling suddenly floods back into my limbs. I see the people walking by and hear them talking. Pan Kov, our neighbor, leans out of her window and calls my name.

But I ignore her. Quietly, I go to the door, walk upstairs, and shut the door to my room.

I sit on my bed and look out the window. I can no longer see the birds flying, but I hear them singing, somewhere far, far up in the summer sky.

And Never Stops at All

It is frigid December weather, and I sit on the floor with Andrej looking through a pile of Christmas seals. We do not celebrate Christmas, but neither do we celebrate Hanukkah, or even go to synagogue. Andrej has brought home his friend's Christmas seals, stamps which are sold for charity, for me to see.

I rub the thin papers in-between my fingers. I am trying to find one with a bird on it.

Someone bangs on the door, loudly. A heavily accented voice barks, "Open up! Now!"

It is a German accent. Tata opens the door and three big, strong Nazis stride into our living room.

"You have fifteen minutes to gather your things," the tallest one snaps. I move closer to Andrej, who stares at the Germans with fire in his eyes. Mama's hand flies to her face. I look around our apartment. This is it? We must simply pick up and go?

Tata tries to reason with the soldiers, but it does no good. We rush around our home, stuffing whatever we can into suitcases. What kind of clothes do we need? Where are we going? How can we just leave?

The soldiers rush us out of our apartment. I look back and see the Christmas seals still scattered on the floor.

"Andrej, your friends seals!"

He shakes his head. Too late.

As we are herded down the stairs, I realize I never found a seal with a bird on it.

And Sweetest in the Gale is Heard

I am surprised to find that spring comes in Terezin just as it came in Prague last year, and the year before, and the year before. Buds are opening on the trees and the sun is smiling down, even on us prisoners. The sky is so blue, it almost makes up for the bedbugs, the scarce food, the many sicknesses, the frightening transports, and the cruelty of the soldiers.

Pan Kov, who lived next to us at home and with us now, somehow smuggled in two books and has been helping me continue to study. I do not much like Pan Kov, for she is loud and excitable. Tata helps me study, too, when he is not working, and Andrej when he is not out with his friends. Andrej has always had many friends, and I have had few. I am nine now and I am glad I can continue my schooling.

I walk down the street, happy because it is so beautifully warm. Tilting my head upwards, I see a bird wheeling in the sky far above me. I squint; it looks blue. Is it a swallow?

A gunshot rings out.

I turn my head in time to see a man crumple to the ground, blood spurting from his head. A German soldier stands over him, cleaning his gun.

I am rooted to the spot. I watch in fascination as the hard-packed soil turns red.

"Amlie! Get away from there!" It is Andrej. He forcefully grabs my arm and drags me down the street. I turn to look back, unable to tear my eyes away. The Nazi catches my gaze and grins wickedly.

Above us, the swallow sings.

Hope is the Thing with Feathers

And Sore Must be the Storm

I have lived in Terezin forever. I cannot remember Prague. I cannot remember my bed, or our apartment, or the tree outside my window, or the swallows that used to perch in it and sing. When I first came to Terezin, I saw many birds, but now I have not seen one in a long, long time. I am ten, and I know now that there are not birds around every corner. I no longer look for them.

I am in the tiny room we live in with Pan Kov, sitting on the floor because Mama and Pan Kov are on the mattresses, pinching the fleas crawling over my legs, and going over my lessons in my head. My arm itches; everywhere itches. At least we are together, I remind myself, as Tata always says. Most families are not.

Tata should be home soon. This is always a highlight of my day, for he brings home funny stories and takes me in his lap to tell them to me. Mama fusses and worries and snaps at Andrej and me all day long, but Tata never does.

The door slams open. I look up. It's Tata. I smile and jump to my feet, ready for a story. But Tata's face is contorted in an expression I have never seen before. He rips off his coat and stomps through the room. Mama and Pan Kov rise, concerned.

"Tata?" I venture. When he whirls around, I see the big purple bruise around his eye.

"We will die in this godforsaken place," my wonderful Tata spits at us viciously. He throws himself onto the mattress and turns his face to the wall.

I sit back down. The fleas crawl over my legs, and I mechanically pinch off their heads.

Hope is the Thing with Feathers

That Could Abash the Little Bird

I have something new to fill my days. Two men named Rudi Freudenfeld and Rafi Schchter are putting on a children's opera, *Brundibar.* They needed more children for the chorus, and I have been chosen!

We have been practicing hard for many months although we are hungry and weak. Soon we shall perform it. We must perform it many times, Pan Schchter says, for it will bring people happiness.

I love the music. I never thought about music in Prague. Someone was always playing music, somewhere, but I never truly listened. Now I am grateful that it drowns out the sound of my growling stomach.

Brundibar is about a brother and sister who sing to earn money for their mother, who is sick. But Brundibar, an evil organ grinder steals the money they make. Many of us children have sick mothers, or no mothers. We understand. When at last Brundibar is defeated, the music swells triumphantly, and I know the audience will cheer and applaud.

I smile as I walk home, with the *Brundibar* music playing in my head.

Home.

In two years that feel like forever, today is the first time I've thought of Terezin as my home and not just where I live.

As I round the corner, heading for our room, a bird flies across the sky.

That Kept So Many Warm

Something odd is happening in Terezin. The Nazis have planted roses. A cafe appears from nowhere. Tata is made to paint fences. Someone whispers it is all for the visit of the Danish Red Cross. They want to check on the Danish Jews, and the Nazis are going to fool them.

I don't know why they are even trying. Of course, the Red Cross will see what is really happening. How could one not see? How could the people dying of typhus and starvation be overlooked? The Germans have put up signs on every corner saying, To the Park, or, To the Baths. Yet there is no park and there are no baths. It is all a lie.

We are to perform for the Red Cross, we who are in *Brundibar*. I prepare for the performance confident that the Red Cross will see our thin faces and demand something be done about it.

When the Germans lead the Red Cross into the community hall, which the Nazis just built, we sing loudly as we have been taught. We have already performed *Brundibar* many times, but surely this will be the last before the Red Cross rescues us. I smile as I sing the lovely music.

When we have finished and Brundibar has been defeated, they clap. Then they stand up and leave.

Weeks later, we hear that the Red Cross returned to Denmark with peace of mind that the Danish Jews were safe. They were completely fooled by the Germans.

I've Heard it in the Chillest Land

I am in our room alone, sitting on the scratchy straw-filled mattress with the *Brundibar* music running through my head. That, and something else: Tata's words. *We will die in this godforsaken place.*

The door opens. Andrej comes in. He turns back to shut the door and then crosses the room. It is so small and his legs have grown so long, it takes him three steps to sit on the mattress beside me. It's funny, how Andrej keeps growing even though there is so little food. Like all of us, he is painfully skinny, but somehow keeps shooting up.

His face is grave and sad. A little angry. I wonder why he is not out with his friends. Usually he does not deign to come home until sundown.

"Where are Gabrjel and the others?" I ask.

He looks at me, appearing to contemplate what to tell me.

"I know everything," I say into silence. "I am no longer a child. You can't hide anything from me. I dont want you to."

"Deported," Andrej says, his voice thick. "They were sent east on one of the transports this morning."

A chill runs up and down my arms. *East.* Rumors about what lies at the end of the train tracks have been flying about Terezin for months. None of them are good.

Andrej turns away. I lean back on the itchy straw and think that perhaps I was wrong. True, I am no longer a child. But neither do I wish to know everything.

And on the Strangest Sea

It is September 1944, and the Nazis are lying again. They are having a Jewish director make a film about the camp. I suppose they will send it to many countries and the people will be fooled just like the Danish Red Cross. I wonder if Kurt Gerron, the Jewish director, will show any birds in the film. Probably not. I still see birds in Terezin, sometimes, most often when I am going home from *Brundibar* rehearsals. But when I point them out to other people, they cannot see them.

We perform *Brundibar* again for the film. When the Red Cross came, I sang loudly and tried to have fun. *Fun.* Then I was still a child, for I naively thought the Red Cross would swoop down and save us all. Now I know better. So I try to look very thin and sad as I sing. If people are going to watch this film, they must open their eyes and see what Terezin really is.

Yet Never in Extremity

The stench is all I can think of. We are on a train, packed in a boxcar, Mama and Tata and Andrej and Pan Kov and I and many other people. There is little air, none of it fresh. No food, no water. We are packed in so tightly, I cannot sit down. We must have been riding for at least a day, perhaps longer. The smell is suffocating. We are headed to that mysterious place, East.

Pan Kov has always been rather loud and brash, easily worried. Now she is nearly hysterical.

"Petra," she whispers harshly, breathing heavily. "Take this."

Mama looks up. Pan Kov is holding out a worn photograph of a man and woman.

"My parents," Pan Kov says in a voice that grows louder with each word. "I smuggled it from Prague to Terezin, and now... keep it for me, Petra, and give it to me afterwards!

Mama looks at the photo for a long time. At last her mouth, which has been set in a straight, hard line for as long as I can remember, softens. She looks at poor Pan Kov, who is practically hyperventilating, with something like pity. Mama takes the picture and slips it into her pocket.

It Asked a Crumb of Me

When we at last stumble off the train into the fresh air, it is dark. I squint. I think I can make out barbed-wire fences, and walking skeletons in striped uniforms. A spotlight shines on a large sign above the gate. *Arbeit macht frei.* I have learned some German in Terezin, and I think this means *work will make you free*. Yet Tata worked hard for years in Terezin, and now we are here.

The German soldiers, holding guns and leashes of large dogs, shove us towards a small building. "Showers," someone says. We are to take showers and then be sent to the barracks.

The crowd pushes and pulls me. I have lost sight of my family. I want to scream. I cannot breathe. I am being trampled.

I look up into the dark sky and see three birds caught in a spotlight. The birds have always been my friends, from Prague to Terezin to here. Auschwitz. I hear again Tata's words. *We will die in this godforsaken place.*

We are herded into the building. People cry out, push, shove, climb on top of one another. The showers turn on, but it is not water.

High above us, the swallows sing around the smokestacks.

About The Author

Hailey Hudson is an eighteen-year-old homeschool grad and a rising college sophomore. She's been obsessed with reading and writing from an early age; other passions of hers include theater, music, traveling, working with kids, eating cheesecake, and playing softball. Hailey is a proud INFJ and a prouder Ravenclaw. Most importantly, she loves Jesus more than anything!

About The Publisher

Story Shares is a nonprofit focused on supporting the millions of teens and adults who struggle with reading by creating a new shelf in the library specifically for them. The ever-growing collection features content that is compelling and culturally relevant for teens and adults, yet still readable at a range of lower reading levels.

Story Shares generates content by engaging deeply with writers, bringing together a community to create this new kind of book. With more intriguing and approachable stories to choose from, the teens and adults who have fallen behind are improving their skills and beginning to discover the joy of reading. For more information, visit storyshares.org.

Easy to Read. Hard to Put Down.

Hope is the Thing with Feathers

www.ingramcontent.com/pod-product-compliance
Lightning Source LLC
Chambersburg PA
CBHW071229170626
46809CB00005BA/1982